Stuart
Armstrong

First published in 2000 by BBC Worldwide Ltd
Woodlands, 80 Wood Lane, London W12 0TT
This edition published in 2003
2 4 6 8 10 9 7 5 3 1
Text by Diane Redmond
Illustrations by Magic Island
Text, design and illustrations © 2000 BBC Worldwide Ltd
Tweenies © 1998 BBC
Tweenies © 1999 BBC Worldwide Ltd
Tweenies is produced by Tell-Tale Productions for the BBC.
CBeebies & logo ™ BBC. © BBC 2002
Printed in Singapore
ISBN 0 563 53298 X

Tweenies™

Happy Birthday, Fizz!

It was Fizz's birthday and, as a special
treat, Judy had taken her to see a ballet.
While they were out, Max helped Bella, Milo
and Jake wrap Fizz's presents. Doodles
watched. He liked birthdays.

"Can I ever have a birthday present?"
Jake asked Max.

"Of course you can," Max replied, and Jake
helped himself to the biggest one!

"No, Jake!" cried Bella. "Today is Fizz's
birthday, not yours, so the presents are
all for her."

Max said that birthdays were extra-special days. Not only did you get presents but you were also another year older.

"Fizz is four years old today," he told them.

The Tweenies helped Max get ready for the party. Milo found the hats and hung up the curly streamers.

Bella blew up the
balloons and Jake helped
Max set the table.

When everything was ready,
they made Fizz a birthday card with
a big number four on the front.

"I've got a great idea," said Milo. "Why don't we stick four candles on Fizz's birthday cake?"

"Oh, yes!" cried Jake.

"Oh, no!" gasped Bella. "We haven't got a cake for Fizz. We forgot to get her a cake!"

But Max hadn't forgotten. The lady next
door had made a cake for Fizz, with pink
icing-sugar ballet shoes.
The Tweenies added four candles.
It was a beautiful cake.

"What a shame
it won't last,"
said Milo.
"Why not?" Jake
asked him.
"Because
we're going
to eat it!"
Milo giggled.

Max said they couldn't eat the cake until Fizz had blown out the candles and made her special birthday wish.

"Oh, I wish I could wish for something," sighed Jake. "Something really big and exciting."

"I know what I'd wish for," said Milo, and he made up a song about it...

"I wish I had a wish, 'cos then I'd wish for a robot to play in the park with me!" he sang.

"I wish I had a wish,
'cos then I'd wish
for a star
to dance in the sky
with me!" sang Bella.

"I wish I had a wish,
'cos then I'd wish
for a dragon
to come and live
with me!" sang Jake.

"I wish I had a wish,
'cos then I'd wish
for sausages
with chops and gravy
for my tea!"
sang Doodles.

When Fizz came back
with Judy, she was
thrilled to see her
party decorations.
"I can't wait to
start my party!"
she cried.

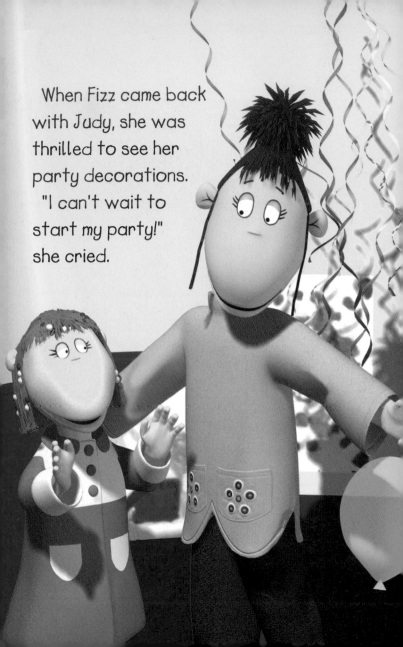

Then Fizz noticed the pink icing-sugar
ballet shoes on the cake.
"What BEAUTIFUL ballet shoes!
I wish..." she began.
But it was time to open the presents.

Bella gave her a jigsaw. Milo's present was a box of coloured crayons.

Jake gave her a big bag of jelly babies. "Thank you, Jake," Fizz said. "We can all share them."

Max and Judy's present
was a song book and a tape.
"We can all sing along
together," said Fizz.

When Judy lit the candles
on the birthday cake, Max said he
knew exactly which song
they should sing.

"Happy birthday to you,
happy birthday to you,
happy birthday, dear Fizz,
happy birthday to YOU!"

Fizz stared at her cake
and made a secret wish.
Then, with one big puff, she
blew out ALL the candles!

Just then, Doodles
raced in with a
parcel for Fizz.
"Woof woof!"
he barked. "Happy
birthday, Fizz!"

"Thank you, Doodles!"
she said. Fizz unwrapped
the present and stared
at it in amazement.

"PINK BALLET SHOES!" she gasped.
"Doodles, you've made my birthday
wish come true!"

THE END